Illustrated by
Max Jackson

Edited by
Hannah Daffern

Published in Great Britain in 2018 by Michael O'Mara Books Limited,
9 Lion Yard, Tremadoc Road, London SW4 7NQ

 www.busterbooks.co.uk   Buster Children's Books   @BusterBooks

A CIP catalogue record for this book is available from the British Library.

HB ISBN: 978-1-78055-531-7
PB ISBN: 978-1-78055-574-4

1 3 5 7 9 10 8 6 4 2

This book was printed in April 2018 by Leo Paper Products Ltd, Heshan Astros Printing Limited,
Xuantan Temple Industrial Zone, Gulao Town, Heshan City, Guangdong Province, China.

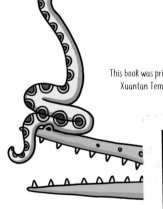

1 · 2 · 3
ANTEATER
stuck up a
TREE

1

silly anteater
is stuck up a tree.

Can you count the other animals
that come along to help him out?

2

curious crocodiles
come to see.

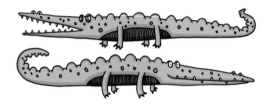

1 anteater

3

friendly moose try
forming a plan.

2 crocodiles
1 anteater

4

sleepy sloths do
all that they can.

3 moose
2 crocodiles
1 anteater

5

slithery snakes try
forming a rope.

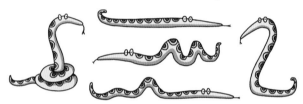

4 sloths
3 moose
2 crocodiles
1 anteater

6

proud flamingos
have given up hope.

5 snakes
4 sloths
3 moose
2 crocodiles
1 anteater

7

lazy bats are just
hanging around.

6 flamingos
5 snakes
4 sloths
3 moose
2 crocodiles
1 anteater

8

loud macaws squawk,
'Climb down to the ground!'

7 bats
6 flamingos
5 snakes
4 sloths
3 moose
2 crocodiles
1 anteater

9

clever frogs have
a great idea ...

8 macaws
7 bats
6 flamingos
5 snakes
4 sloths
3 moose
2 crocodiles
1 anteater

10

tiny ants suddenly appear!

9 frogs
8 macaws
7 bats
6 flamingos
5 snakes
4 sloths
3 moose
2 crocodiles
1 anteater

The ants are marching quietly by,
when all of a sudden they
catch someone's eye ...

CRASH!

... they all fall down.

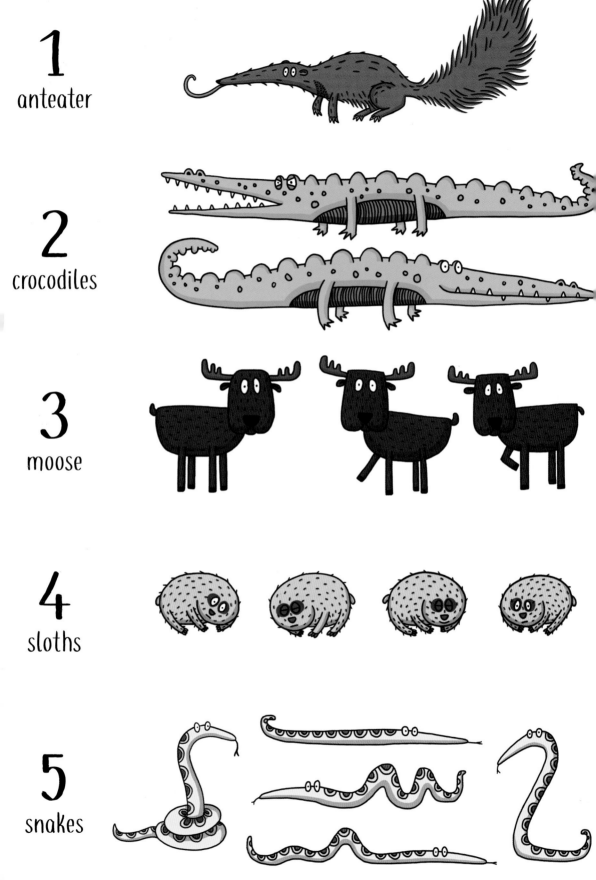

1 anteater

2 crocodiles

3 moose

4 sloths

5 snakes

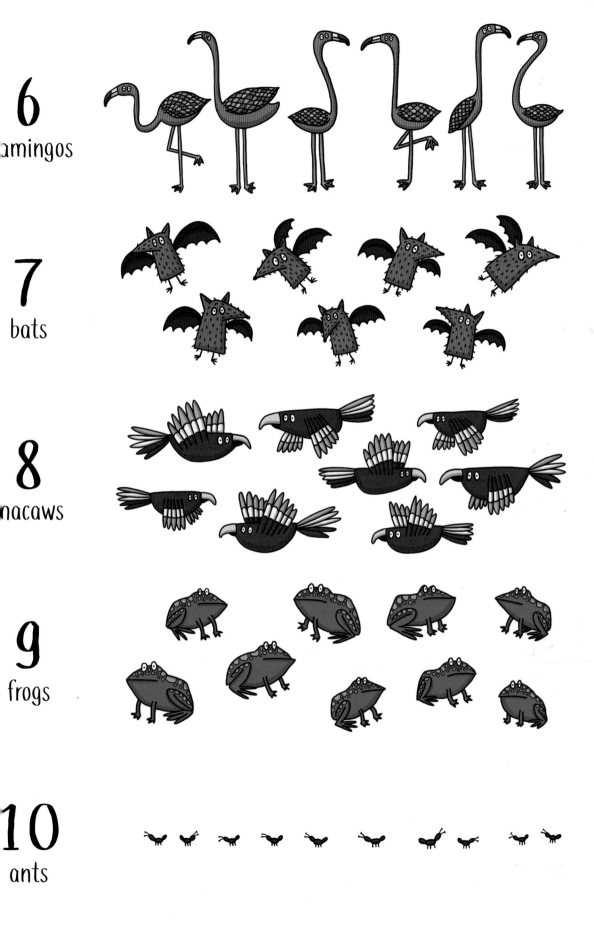

6 flamingos

7 bats

8 macaws

9 frogs

10 ants